The

Christmas Miracle

Of

Castle Neuschwanstein

Marion Wittrowski

The Christmas Miracle

of

Castle Neuschwanstein

About giving a little and getting so much in return …

Impressum:

© 2011 Marion Wittrowski

Cover creation: Klaus Wittrowski

Pictures: bigstockphoto

English Translation: Bettina Blandin

Production and Publisher: Books on Demand
GmbH, Norderstedt

ISBN: 978-3-839137-87-1

A Time of Contemplativeness and Miracles

Dear Readers.

This book really means a lot to me.

It is about a very touching Christmas Story. Every Christmas the bailiff couple of Castle Neuschwanstein, not having children of their own, takes care of homeless persons, especially children. This year however, things are different, for the first time problems occur.

Christmas time is about giving, not about taking. What really is the sense of Christmas? It is about helping other people who are having a hard time. It is about love among the people, about charity. You do not need to be rich to be in a position to give someone a helping hand and invite him to spend a couple of hours among friends. What does our dining table look like on Christmas Eve? Plenty of appetizing starters, roasts, side dishes and desserts. A lot of people would be grateful for a hot soup on a cold winter's day.

Just give a little of what you have got and make a person happy. Fill other people's hearts with some warmth and love, and let the miracle happen.

I wish you a contemplative Christmas among your family.

Yours,

Marion Wittrowski

What a fantastic view, the castle seems to grow out of the rock. It seems been built by a sugar baker.

Snow everywhere, the landscape seems to be covered with sugar powder. The first sunrays bathe the castle in an ocean of colours. So powerful as if the sun wants to occupy it totally and exclusively. Everything seem so peacefully, so inviting and romantic. The Pöllat Canyon under the bridge "Marienbrücke" is covered with ice and reminds a fairy tale. You almost expect elves or fairies paltering on the rock face.

Richard is shaking his head: "So here I am standing on the bridge as I have been every day for 30 years, always thinking about the same."

A handsome man in his mid-fifties, Richard is standing on the bridge, lost in thought. His hair and beard already turned grey, shine like silver in the sun. He is looking at the castle. "There is no other place in the world I would rather be", he thinks to himself, a content smile on his still tanned face.

Richard administers the Castle Neuschwanstein, built 1886 by King Ludwig. He and his wife Resi are living in a big flat in the bower, the three-storey building between the courtyard and the canyon. That is where his office is located, from where he manages without any effort all the small and big problems.

Resi, a small woman with a little overweight looks after every single helper who cares for the castle. There are some twenty guides in the main season, now in winter they need only ten. In December, there is an average of 4000 daily visitors who want to be guided through the castle. There is also the cleaning team, numerous men and women from the surrounding towns like Schwangau and Füssen, who have to clean up after the tourists. Two craftsmen carry out small repairs. Franz, an elderly man in his sixties, is close to Resi's heart. His wife died one year ago and he seems not to be able to get over it. Franz controls the 15 monitors standing in a small room aside the office. From there he can keep every room in the castle under surveillance. Resi provides him every day with lunch and takes half an hour time to listen to his stories about his wife. For the other members of the group she would bake cakes or cookies and also let them tell her about their worries or weekend adventures. Resi listens to everybody and they all make use of it. Although Resi is two heads smaller than her husband Richard, she is treated with the same respect. With her resolute manners, her always-friendly looking brown eyes and dimples, she puts a spell on everyone. Her dark brown hair with silver strands here and there, dressed into a thick braid and her rosy face give her a country folk look.

Most of the people think she has the heart in the right place. She is extremely intelligent and knows very well what she wants. They are certainly right.

Richard sighs as he leaves the bridge (Marienbrücke). Although it is bitterly cold up here in December, he is making the rounds every morning at 6 o'clock. First he peers the upper, then the lower courtyard. Then he continues through the castellated gateway. The rounds always end at the bridge 600 meters afar, where the view over the castle is unique.

This is where Richard stays every day thanking God for his wonderful wife and for his singular home.

He smells coffee when he passes the door. As every morning, Resi set the table up. Fresh bread rolls, scrambled eggs and baked ham compose a rather substantial meal for this hour of the day but Resi insists on eating well before starting the day.

Richard takes off the coat with the fur lining and puts it on a chair, and then he rubs the coffee can with his frozen fingers to warm them up.

„Oh Richard, once more you just threw your coat on the chair. What's up? We have a coat rack, put it over there. And again you didn't put your gloves on".

„Okay, Resi, tomorrow I will take the gloves, just to please you", Richard calms her down.

„You shouldn't do it for me, but because of your rheumatism. This evening you will not be able to move your fingers and start complaining again", answers Resi.

Richard pours himself a cup of coffee and decides not to go into details. She is right, but he would not admit it.

This morning was about Christmas. They could not have children of their own and therefore care every Christmas for children of the neighbourhood, orphans and homeless people.

She reminds Richard of his duties: "Richard, only five days left till Christmas and we still do not have any tree. Would you please get one today!"

"I will, but this evening. We are expecting some tourist groups from Japan and America today. We will need a lot of Ludwig posters and I still have to unpack them. Moreover, one guide got sick; I will certainly have to replace him. But later on I will get the tree", Richard explains to her.

Every Christmas Eve they invite 10 children to give them some feeling of security and love.

A ceremony is planned as every year. Resi has been baking cookies for days, organizing covers, warm clothes and toys in the village. Everything was lovingly gift-wrapped and will be put under the tree.

This year homeless children sleeping rough with their parents will come. "It is so frosty, we need real warm clothes for the children", Resi says out loud her thoughts.

He nods his head, finishes eating and puts on his jacket. The first tourists are expected at 10 o'clock, everything has to be ready by then. "His" castle must be nice and tidy and shine in old splendour. He has to supervise in order to prevent sloppy work.

The castle receives more than 1 million visitors every year. It has to be spring-cleaned to avoid a fading of the former glamour.

Richard goes through the rooms, looks in every corner and checks the floors. Everything is perfect today. He decides to get his coat and go to the turnaround. This is the terminal stop for the carriages bringing the tourists as near as possible to the castle. Wolfgang, the tenant of the kiosk located there is his friend and always pleased to see him.

As Richard comes in the apartment to get his coat, he hears Resi speaking. Out of here, she is again speaking on the phone with some people about donations. If she pinched him, he would have to drive to the village to pick up those things. He really does not feel like it. He catches the coat and escapes. He only puts the coat on when he reaches the stairs outside the bower, and then he heads to Wolfgang who is glad to see him. "The coffee is almost ready, sit down", Wolfgang invites his guest. He always comes very early to sort the newspapers, clean and place in new merchandise. But he always has time for a chat when Richard comes.

Enjoying his cup of hot coffee, Wolfgang wants to know the state of affairs concerning Christmas Eve.

"Well you know, as every year it gets quite chaotic. Resi is always on the phone, constantly occupied with baking and pushing me around. *Go get the provisions, think of the Christmas Tree, one of the fairy lights broke down, get the drinks and so on"* Richard responds amused. "As soon as I have the time, I'm going to feel sorry for you", Wolfgang teases his friend.

"I think it's great what Resi gets going every year. By the way, I have some boxes here you might take with you later on. This year I am donating sweets, paper bags and gift-wrap paper. This evening I will bring two crates of orange-coke mix. Tell Resi so she might cancel such things from her list", Wolfgang says with a smile.

"You are a real friend, giving me even more work, but it is ok, I will tell her", Richard is joking.

"Will you come on Christmas Eve, or do you have a new girlfriend?" Richard enquires with caution. Wolfgang is in his early fifties, quite handsome, has a full head of curly brown hair and he is in shape, he has never been married. He usually succeeds in approaching the young temporary employees hired in summer. Sometimes the flirt goes on till the next year. He would not spend Christmas with Richard and Resi in this case.

I'm a single this year, but I will meet an old schoolmate in Munich. I won't join you this year", Wolfgang replies. "What's wrong Wolfgang? No queen of your heart this year? Are you getting old?", Richard is teasing. "Me, old? Nonsense! I just did not meet the one", Wolfgang explains.

Both continue to joke a while, then Richard leaves the kiosk in direction of the castle. He drops by to see Resi and then opens the castle. During wintertime, the castle closes at 4 o'clock, and he has more time for important tasks or private life.

Resi is just phoning with the supermarket in Füssen in order to organize food and sweets. Richard pours himself a cup of coffee, waiting for his wife to hang up.

"Can you imagine, we get so many donations this year that we can even invite the children's parents." Resi is completely stoked. It is very cold this year and she also wants to procure a nice warm evening to the adults. Resi always gets done what she resolves to do. "If you go on like this, we will soon have the castle full of people. You cannot shelf the tramps of the whole world", Richard reminds her. "Not all, but as many as possible. See how frosty it is outside, and it is even starting to snow. Can you imagine how these poor people actually suffer, how they freeze without having anything to be happy about? How they try to protect their children from the cold even when they are hungry? I just have to do this, can't you understand me Richard?"

"It is ok Resi. Do not get upset, that was quite brainless from my part. Of course, we will make as many persons as possible happy on that day. But what about the day after when they have to go back to the cold, won't they be even more unhappy?", Richard enquires with caution.

"I've been thinking about this for quite some time. But I do hope that they will feed of this one day we offer them. Maybe the feeling of not being alone in this world will give them courage – when they notice that there are people who care about others, when they perceive that the sense of Christmas is not yet lost. They might draw new hope." Resi's is getting sad.

"Don't be sad Resi. Everything will turn out right. Let's believe in miracles, they might occur in Christmas time", Richard comforts his wife. "I should tell you that Wolfgang sends sweets, paper bags and gift wrap paper to you, I already put the box in the vestibule. And he will bring two crates of orange-coke mix this evening by himself. I'll get the rest this afternoon, is that ok?"

Resi nods her head. "Yes it is. But please think of the Christmas tree, it has to be decorated tomorrow, otherwise I won't get everything done in time", she reminds him. Richard puts his cup back on the table and gets up for the next round through the castle.

The first tours are already over, and there always was something to be done.

Resi continues her cookies. This year she needs more than usually as there will be many adults.

Meanwhile Richard gets to the throne room. What was that? Some chocolate bar wrapping paper on the marble stairs leading to the inexistent throne. What kind of people are they who just stamp through without appreciating the majestic beauty?

For King Ludwig the castle was not only the location of the royal representation but also a place of withdrawal from his world dominated by strange thoughts. It was the place he came to escape in an poetic dream world, always searching for romance in his life. The swan was the heraldic animal, the Christian symbol of the immaculate ness King Ludwig aimed for. If he saw how it looked like after the tours, he would turn over in his grave.

While Richard wanders on the paths of the past, Resi is facing reality. On Christmas Eve 18 persons will stand there full of expectations, and she still has so many things to get done. Everything should be perfect. Every single of those 18 persons shall receive a big bag containing home-made cookies, fruit, cold cuts, bread and cheese. Furthermore the gifts must be wrapped and the tree decorated. No doubt,

Richard has to help. But where is he again? Probably wandering through the castle for the fifth time, picking up paper scraps.

Resi starts to prepare lunch. She takes a plate and sets forth to Franz. He certainly is hungry, it already is far past noon.

Resi apologizes for being so late. Nobody in the castle resents to her, everyone knows the nearer Christmas comes, the more she has to do.

Franz enjoys the knuckle of pork with the sauerkraut and regales himself. Resi does not have to look for Richard who is standing near Franz, watching the tourists on the monitors, still searching the one who drop the paper scrap. After a little chat with Franz, Resi goes to have lunch with Richard.

During the meal, Richard enquires with caution about the Christmas festivity for the employees, which shall take place on December 22nd. Bad timing, he should have chosen another moment. Now he is blamed for not helping enough and asked how Resi should get everything done alone. Richard is given a strict plan of what he has to do. That is what he ended up with.

First the lounge has to be decorated for the employees' festivity. Richard should do it this afternoon together with two or three of the staff. But the decoration must be picked up in the basement before.

Resi wants to join them later and help. But primarily the gifts must be wrapped. Everyone gets a nice cookie jar full of homemade cookies and a Christmas card with Richard's and Resi's best wishes.

Richard strays off topic by relating about the paper scrap in the throne room and his usual indignation. Resi however has other problems. The food for the meal on the 22nd must be picked up in the village, there still are neither candles nor napkins. How should she get all this done? Every year Resi is making such a fuss about it and finally all turns out right. The meal always starts without delay, the gifts use to lie under the tree and the festivity is ever so beautiful. Everybody is happy and looking forward to two days off, on every December 24th and 25th the castle remains closed.

"You really want to send me down the mountain to the village with this weather?", Richard asks. "How should all the food and first of all our Christmas tree come up here?" Resi starts to be really angry. "All right, as soon as we close I will go", Richard appeases her.

The castle's idyllic situation is unique. Up high on the mountain, it towers majestically over the small town Hochschwangau. Tourists who want to visit the castle have to leave their cars in the village. They can continue by foot, steep uphill, take a transfer bus or choose a horse-drawn carriage. In winter, it is a very special experience to go by carriage through the snow-covered forest. There is nothing more romantic.

Richard is the only one to be allowed to go by car, and it helps a lot for the provisioning with food. He hits the road after 4 o'clock, being a little morose. It has been snowing continuously for an hour, the way down to the village is tiring. The castle closing at 4 o'clock, the snow ploughs come rather late – in case they do come at all – to shift the snow off the way. When there is a lot of it and the village has to be cleared, they come only in the early morning. If Richard or Resi then want to go down the mountain, they have to call and wait till a plough clears their way.

Richard drives carefully and slowly, it takes him a long time to reach Hohenschwangau. He picks up the shopping Resi ordered by phone the morning and enjoys a coffee at his friends' Alois, owner of the local bakery. They talk a little about the weather, not more, because hell broke loose in the shop so short before

Christmas. He returns to Resi. Meanwhile the way has been cleared so he is back fast as the wind.

Resi prepares the dinner whilst Richard carries the shopping in the house. "Will you bring the tree in the house after the meal?", Resi asks. "For heaven's sakes, I totally forgot it"; Richard is looking quite guilty.

Resi sets the table, she prefers to keep silent now. Richard is worried.

He would have preferred her to rail at him. When she does not speak at all she is ever so mad. Richard gets up quickly, takes his jacket and says while leaving: "I'll be right back!" The door claps and Resi is alone again. She smiles. „So what", she thinks. If she had railed at him, Richard would certainly have gone only tomorrow to get the tree. Now he has bad conscience and the tree will be here this evening.

Richard drives to the only market garden in Hohenschwangau to pick up the ordered tree. This makes him notice that the tree for the lounge was not picked up either. So they put both trees on the bed of his pickup. Peter, the owner of the market garden donates two trees every year. Most of the time the tree for the lounge is picked up by one of the drivers. It usually is Thomas' job, but he got sick.

So Richard takes the tree to the castle. He is back there after half an hour and they can have dinner. Resi does not even mention it, being happy that the tree finally arrived. After the meal Richard erects first the tree in the living room, then the one in the lounge. Rather difficult to do, as both trees are some two and a half meters high. Resi has to help him. They are done at about 8 o'clock.

Resi decides to postpone the decoration to the next day, for today that was it. They both sit down on the sofa with a glass of wine and watch a thriller on TV before going to bed.

They already get up at 5 o'clock the next morning. Richard goes for his rounds. As usual Resi prepares a copious breakfast. Today both trees are being decorated, a festoon of pine branches and fabric boots are put on the chimney, then Resi helps to decorate the lounge.

There are not so many tours foreseen for tomorrow, anyhow it is getting less from day to day. So Richard can cool down a bit. He relieves Resi of the lunch transport for Franz, goes to see Wolfgang in his kiosk and has even enough time to help Resi to fill the cookie jars. A quite peaceful day comes to its end. In the evening Resi gives some phone calls to complete the donations, she asks some friends for help.

They care about cakes and guest beds and promise to bring the things over. Richard and Resi let the day die away with a cup of hot spiced wine.

On the 22nd Richard is awaken by a loud bang at 4 o'clock in the morning. He jumps out of his bed, being sure that something awful occurred in the castle. It would not be the first time the lustre in the throne room falls from the ceiling. But as Richard enters the kitchen he finds out what happened. Resi is already pottering around, and as she wanted to take a big white china jar out of the kitchen cabinet it fell on the floor and smashed to smithereens. That is too much, Resi starts crying. „Oh Resi, what's the matter? No problem, we will buy another one", Richard tries to comfort his wife. "You know, I just break everything I touch. Yesterday I dropped the angel of the treetop. I got it from my mother, and it is also broken in tiny pieces. And today my mother's cookie jar. It is all things you just can't replace", Resi sobs. Richard takes his wife in his arms to comfort her and asks why she is in the kitchen at 4 o'clock in the morning. He finds out that she has already been baking for two hours. Richard does not try to talk her out such behaviour any more.

As Resi calms down again, they sweep the shards away and sit down in the dining room with a cup of coffee and wonderful smelling warm cookies. The view over the mountains from there is fantastic, but only as long as there is daylight. So they watch the stars in the sky.

Then everything runs like clockwork. At half past four everything is ready for the employees' festivity and everyone curls up. Richard delivers a little speech, thanking everybody for the good teamwork during this year. At the end of the party all thank Resi for the beautiful Christmas party and promise to help on the 24th wherever they can. This evening Resi falls asleep, satisfied with herself and everything else.

The next morning however, she is not so relaxed anymore. The stress is already starting at five o'clock. Richard gets order by order. Resi established a list he has to complete this very day. Breakfast was shorter than usual, no more calm in the house now. Twenty tours still were to take place. Franz should come to the house for the meal and most of the employees had to be seen off with the best wishes for Christmas.

In Resi's kitchen all morning food is being snipped, cleaned, prepared and cooked. And still baking activities are going on. When Richard and Franz come for lunch at half past one, the kitchen is upside down.

The tours are over for this day, everything cleared and the people Resi would not meet again the next day wanted to say goodbye in all this chaos. Little gifts for Resi and Richard are brought, help is offered to them but they deny. All those who do not live in the castle leave. Only Franz is still sitting there in his blue uniform, he is the security guard at least, you have to notice when seeing him. It does not really happen, as he only leaves his small monitor room to have his meal with Resi, but it makes him feel important.

"Franz, will you join us tomorrow?", Resi asks him. "With pleasure, so I won't be alone at home. Should I bring something?" Franz is on cloud nine. He had already been afraid of this Christmas Eve as it is the first since his wife died. He is relieved not to be alone, the children would be a beautiful distraction.

"Nice, so you might help me with the children. They have to be occupied in the meantime. You could for example play games with Richard and the children." Resi is very pleased.

Richard wants to leave, he still has his list of things to get done. Franz takes the opportunity to accompany him down to the village, so he does not have to walk. It is still snowing. Although the ploughs were there in the morning, snow is again everywhere.

Richard has to drive carefully to avoid sliding. He drops Franz at his home and continues alone.

First stop is the big supermarket in Füssen. They already packed all donations in boxes. Fritz, the owner, is an old schoolmate of Rosi and donates a lot every year. He gets a big jar of homemade cookies in return. Franz and Richard charge the boxes, then Richard continues to the little store. The owner heard of the project three years ago and offered her help to Resi. Those boxes are also ready.

She cordially welcomes Richard, enquires about Resi, and the boxes are added to the ones on the bed. "I put some duvet jackets, warm pullovers, kids trousers, scarves, caps and gloves. I hope the sizes fit more or less", the store's boss lady explains the multitude of boxes. "That will be fine. Thank you and Merry Christmas", Richard's says good-bye to her. So says she and hello to Resi, and Richard drives back to Hohenschwangau. There he has to meet his friend Anton, the one with the small supermarket in the village.

He also has some donations, among those fruit, sparkling water, jam, tea and small toys for the children. As those boxes are on the bed. Richard decides to cover it with a tarpaulin. It is snowing more and more, the boxes will not stand it.

Anton helps to fix the tarpaulin, then they take leave of each other. They would meet the next evening anyhow. Anton uses to come with his wife, as some other people of the village, in order to help Resi and Richard.

He drives on to the butcher shop Gerster from where they get every year meat and cold cuts. In the Restaurant „Königliche Stube" pots filled with potato salad and chicken breast were prepared. Richard thanks and also leaves a jar of Resi's cookies.

On we go to Landhaus Müller. The lady boss is pleased to see Richard and gives him a piece of Bavarian meat loaf as refreshment. Then they talk about the next day, how many persons are to be fed and Resi's big heart. Richard gets some dishes of pudding, twenty chicken legs and an entire box of chocolate Santa Claus. Richard leaves again a jar and continues his way.

His last stop is the bakery of his good friend Alois. They have been friends since school time. Every week they meet at the regular's table in the small village pub.

„Hi Alois, Resi sends me. Have you got something for her?", Richard asks his friend. "Sure, I wouldn't forget it and make Resi angry", Alois jokes. "You seem frozen, would you like some hot coffee?" – "Yes I would, even a big cup and nice hot". – „Here you are.

How are things going on the mountain?", Alois asks. „Well, like every year Resi is totally hectic and completely bugged out. This year she even invited the children's parents. So we'll have eighteen persons and she doesn't get through with baking cookies", Richard explains to his friend. "I know how many persons will come, I'm finally in charge of the guest list", Alois responds.

"That's right! You choose the people. Where do you get the names from?" Richard asks. "This year I provide the buns and yesterday's left-over cake to the homeless, so I know them and their stories quite well. This year I choose only hardship cases, we'll take care of the others tomorrow evening. I got some bags of cookies we made in the bake house for Resi. That should be enough. Tell her to stop baking", Alois responds. "Resi and you could become the saviours of the world", Richard says. "That's not our aim. We only want to give some people of our region a little love and hope", Alois responds relaxed. Richard feels guilty for having been so ironic.

Luckily the men of the snow clearing services arrive for a coffee and distract Alois. Richard turns to them. „Hi guys, how far is the work?" he asks. "From here we go to the castle, we'll clear the way for you", one of them answers.

"Fine, then I wait here till you are back. With all the snow fallen during the last two hours I won't take the risk to go up." – "Give us half an hour, then you can go on without any danger", the other man says.

Richard thanks the men by paying their coffee. He still has enough time to buy a Christmas present for Resi. He always does it on the eleventh hour. But what should he give to her? She finally has got everything, but suddenly he has an idea. Richard goes to the small gift shop at the end of the street. He buys a magnificent tinsel angel and leaves the shop sure to have found the perfect Christmas present. Back at Alois' both men charge the boxes in the car and Richard drives on the cleared way up to the castle.

Resi puts the food away and checks the clothes, toys and sweets. All is being sorted so that everybody gets about the same.

It is a hectic December 23rd. In the castle they cook, decorate, wrap gifts, extend and set the big table in the dining room.

Resi likes to be ready early so she still has time for friends and to run some errands. Everything is done at ten o'clock. She prepares tea, takes a plate with cookies and sits down at Richard's side in the living room.

"Richard, don't you think we are really happy? We have our income, an extraordinary home and great friends. We should be grateful." – "That's what I am Resi, I really am. But first of all I am thankful to be married with you." They cuddle up to each other on the sofa and let their minds wander.

They wake up very early on the next morning, December 24th. Looking out of the window they notice that it has been snowing all night long. They can see the town and the mountains from there. Everything looks so peaceful, as if during the night God had sugared it to please them.

Richard prepares the chimney for the evening while Resi fixes breakfast. It should be cuddly when the guests arrive. They have a copious breakfast today as later on they would not have time to eat. Resi worries about homeless people. She asks herself where they stay with this kind of weather? She is happy the people are already been brought to the castle at four o'clock. Some villagers agreed to bring the children and their parents up the mountain.

Resi checks the guest rooms. Eighteen persons will need a place to sleep. Everything is perfect. Only the ducks have not been prepared, but there is still time to do so. When they hear the snow ploughs they go down to the village.

Every year at ten o'clock the friends meet in Alois' bakery to have hot spiced wine, hot chocolate and appetizers.

As they arrive in the village they perceive that something's wrong. Police and ambulance vehicles are on the market place, there is utter confusion.

In the moment a black car is arriving on the market place they notice that something very bad must have happened. Two policemen try to calm down two children who start screaming and struggling at the sight of the black car. When Resi sees that, she runs towards the policemen. What is happening there is inhuman, she has to help the children. "What's the matter?" she asks the policeman shortly. „They are homeless, the parents perished by cold last night and we want to bring the children in an orphanage", the policeman willingly informs her.

Resi starts being angry. What? The children just lost their parents. They could not deal with the situation and should now be brought in an orphanage? On Christmas Eve? She urgently had to do something. "We are taking the children with us with us in the bakery, so they can drink a cup of hot chocolate and warm themselves up, then we will see", Resi says resolutely.

"Impossible! The people from the Public Welfare will be here in a minute", the police officer asks to consider. "I take the children with me. When those people arrive, they can get in touch with me in the bakery. I will talk with them." There is something in Resi's voice not admitting any contradiction. She takes the children by the hands and disappears with them in the bakery "Alois".

The police officer is pretty much at a loss, what should he do? "Well, I'd rather wait for the Public Welfare. Better let them deal with her", he thinks, shrugging his shoulders. He goes back to work not wanting to take on this resolute woman on Christmas Eve.

Meanwhile Resi goes with the children to Alois' kitchen and gives them hot chocolate and buns. The little girl is charming. Her blond curly hair and her puppet face make her look like an angel. She sits at the table without touching anything. The boy is more athletic than his sister. He shoves a bun in her face, saying "You must eat it, it's good for you." The little girl looks so fragile you want to protect her. Her brother also seems to. After some time she takes the bun and finishes it. Both eat all they can find on the table. It seems they did not eat for a long time. Resi reminds them to slow down, but they ignore it.

Resi hopes that they won't feel queasy and wonders if their little stomach might cope with it.

"I am Resi, what are your names?" she casually enquires. The boy assumes the answer: "My name is Josef, and my sister's Maria". "Oh, how beautiful names"; Resi thinks, and how perfect meeting Maria and Josef on Christmas Eve. What does that mean?"

"And how old are you", she wants to know. "I am eight and Maria is five", he answers decently. "Where are Mummy and Daddy?" Maria asks whiningly. Resi has no time to say something, Josef answers right away: "They are dead. I just told you." – "And when will they come back?" Maria insists. Resi takes over before he has the time to act no sensitively again. "Mummy and Daddy are in heaven with God. They will watch you from above now", Resi tries to calm down the child. "Oh, that's fine. Mummy already explained me, they will get wings and watch me when I'm sleeping." It is good Maria found her own explanation.

Richard also arrives in the bakery. He had looked around outside and found out what happened. He takes place to warm himself up with a cup of coffee. "What an icy wind", he thinks.

Two women come in the bakery and ask for the children. Alois shows her the way to the kitchen.

"Good evening, my name is Berta Schreiner from the Public Welfare. This is my colleague Sabine Wimmer. We come to take the children to the orphanage. Ah, here you are. Come with us, we will take you to a warm place where you can play with a lot of other children", the hard-looking elderly woman requests without further explanation. Her colleague, Sabine Wimmer, a very young woman with the hair styled in a chignon seems to be new in the business. She stays behind the strong and tall Mrs. Schreiner and stares at the floor.

"Good evening, I am Resi Brunner, and I think you should not take the children to the orphanage on Christmas Eve. Isn't it hard enough that they lost their parents? Should they even go to an orphanage?" Resi bristles with anger. „It's not our decision, there is a law, I'm sorry for you Mrs. Brunner. Or are you a near relative?" Mrs. Schreiner asks without emotion. „No, I'm just a concerned citizen, keeping the children's well-being in mind". Resi gets real angry. "What kind of people are they, dealing so cold with two small kids"; she asks herself.

Josef puts his arm around his little sister and appeases her: "Don't be afraid Maria. I'll take care of you, nothing will happen to you."

This is the limit for Resi. What a courage this little boy has! She gives a questioning look to her husband. He understands her without any words and nods his head, giving the go-ahead to her.

"Listen to me, you Public-Welfare-broads, it's Christmas Eve and those kids won't be taken to any orphanage as long as I'm around, should I come for the mayor. Got me?" Resi's voice does not allow any opposition. One thinks that if even only one of the "Public-Welfare-broads" dares entering an objection, Resi would hit her with a frying pan. "You are here to act for the children's good and what are you doing? You frighten them to death!"

Mrs. Schreiner does not seem to notice the danger coming from Resi and takes a deep breath to go on the counter attack. But Richard sees the red light and intervenes. "Please excuse my wife's exhalation, she's always sensible during Christmas time if it's about altruism. But she is right, the children can by no means go to the orphanage today. If you agree, we'll take the children to our home for the holidays. We will take care of them", Richard says gravely. "And by the way, she didn't want to affront you by calling you Public-Welfare-broads", he continues, showing a sharp look at Resi. Resi bites the bullet and voices a kind of excuse under her breath.

Both children nestle to Resi as if they want to shelter from Mrs. Schreiner who seems quite angry. Resi puts both arms around Josef and Maria so they feel secure.

A little voice comes from behind Mrs. Schreiner. Behold – Mrs. Wimmer also has something to say. "Berta, I believe it would match. Don't you think it would be the best for the children?" Mrs. Schreiner frowns, considering whether she should forgive this woman having called them "Public-Welfare-broads" or not. Finally, her common sense takes over. What would her Christmas Eve be if she had to start looking for places in the orphanage? And all that paperwork! "Fine then, we will come over after the holidays and decide what to do. I need your personal data, for the sake of good order", Mrs. Schreiner chunters.

The formalities completed they sit down for a while with their friends who also lovingly take care of the children. Resi sneaks out and goes right to the toyshop on the other side of the road. She buys a cuddly white bear with a Christmas hat for Maria and a nostalgic red truck for Josef. Then she goes to a shop where she looks for children's clothes. They should wear something new this evening. Resi estimates their sizes. A jacket, two pants, two pullovers and some underwear for Josef; a dress, a trouser, a jacket, underwear and two pullovers for Maria. She gets it done in very short time, puts the bags in the car, then goes to Alois to fetch the children. They also need shoes. The ones they are wearing now are burst, and that with all the snow! When she enters the room, Josef hugs her. "Thank you that you saved us from the orphanage. You will even not notice we are there", the little boy stammers. He takes his sister by the hand and also tanks Richard for the saving.

Then they go to buy shoes, boots and slippers. The children cannot believe it – new shoes, they did not get some for an eternity

They go back to the bakery where the children get an orange-coke mix while Resi talks with Gerda, Alois' wife. Gerda a slim humorous wife in her prime brims is over with enthusiasm for the children. "What else should I get for this evening?", she asks Resi. "Maybe some toys to divert them, or some clothes", Resi suggests. „Do you know their sizes?", Gerda enquires. „I'll make you a note of it". Resi takes a slip of paper and writes it down. Then she joins the others in the kitchen.

They say good-by to their friends and apologize that the Christmas party will this year take place without them. Everybody understands it, no question.

On the way to the castle, Resi caresses Richard saying "I knew Christmas would leave its mark on you."

As they arrive in the castle, the children are flabbergasted. "You live in a real castle?" Maria asks with excitement. "Yes we do. It is not our own, but we watch over it", Richard answers.

While Richard shows everything to the children Resi prepares the clothes pressing room, all other rooms being already occupied this evening. Then they unpack together the clothes Resi bought for them. Maria brims over with enthusiasm for her new dress and wants to put it on right away. But Resi does not allow it. "First you take a bath and then a rest. We are expecting a lot of guests this evening, you should be well-rested", Resi stops her. After the bath they get a banana and a glass of milk. They fall asleep clean, full and completely exhausted.

Resi takes care of the dinner, she has a lot of hungry mouths to feed this evening. When the ducks are in the oven, Richard says: "Resi, we have to talk." His serious look means nothing good. "What's wrong? I still have so much work before our guests arrive." Richard notices that she wants to get around the discussion. "Doris and Gerda will help. Everything is under control. Sit down. If you think postponing solves the problem, you are wrong", Richard says vigorously.

Resi knows that she cannot avoid the question and says to herself "Better talk now". "Richard, there is nothing to talk about, I want to keep the children." – "There is quite a lot to talk about, my dear. It affects me as much as you. I already had the impression at Alois' that you feel too concerned. Now I notice that I was right. Remember that we are not so young any more. What about the children if something happens to us? Should they go through the same thing once more? And who will then take care of them? Will we be able to manage the situation? When they start to realize that their parents are dead, will we be able to help them? There are psychologists in the orphanage who would take care. Are we still young enough to stand the phase of puberty? Our daily routine would change completely." Richard talks non-stop to Resi.

„Stop it Richard. We are not too old to raise two children. At least they are no babies. They will sleep all night without needing neither nappies nor baby bottles. And yes they lost their parents, this is the decisive point. How do you think they would care for them in the orphanage? Do you believe they always have time to give them comfort them when they need it most? There are so many other children who need love and care.

You know how I would have loved to have children of my own, but we could not have any. Is it our destiny? Is God fulfilling my biggest wish? I don't ask you to adopt the children right away. We could offer to be the foster family and then we see. Please let's at least try!" Resi ends with a trusty look at Richard.

Richard just cannot deny Resi's request when she is looking at him this way. "Okay, we try, but as foster family. We'll talk to Mrs. Schreiner after the holidays and see what will happen", Richard gives in. "Thank you Richard, I love you." She hugs her husband and disappears in the kitchen even before he can say something.

Richard thinks about Resi, he would not want to change her. She has the heart in the right place, that's why he loves her so much. Should he try to give a very special Christmas present to her? "I have to go down to the village again, I'll be right back", he calls out to her. As he leaves he collides with Gerda and Doris. "Not so vehement, young man", Gerda jokes. "I've got something to do", he says. Then he disappears. Both women look at each other and shrug their shoulders. Doris wonders what he is having in mind. They go in the kitchen to help Resi to prepare everything for the evening.

Resi wakes the children up. They have to get dressed, the guests will soon arrive.

"Where is Richard again? I need him, I have to change clothes and make myself presentable", she says to herself. "Go ahead, we have everything under control", Gerda quiets her.

A little later they hear the sound of snow crunching underfoot and a babble of voices. That means the guests are on the way up. Resi fetches the children and they go to welcome the guests on the door. "But look who!" Richard is among all the strangers, and he brought Franz along. The drivers get hot spiced wine and cookies. As every year Richard cares about the friends setting forth to take the Christmas guests up. Richard throws his coat on the coat rack and kicks off.

In the meantime Resi and the children welcome the newcomers with a cup of hot chocolate. "Aunt Resi, why are all these people here?", Maria asks curiously. "They all come to celebrate Christmas with us", Resi answers. – "But Mummy and Daddy are not coming, right?", Maria asks sadly. "No my darling, they won't come. They will look at you from heaven above and will always be in your hearts", Resi tries to quiet the little girl.

Josef is very silent and thoughtful. Resi wonders what is going on in his little head. But no time for thinking, she has to entertain the guests.

Richard also helps now. He just saw the drivers off thanking and wishing Merry Christmas to them.

The meal is a raving success again. Everybody is unrestrained and joyous. How happy they all look, as if there was no tomorrow with hunger and cold. No thinking in tomorrow. Today they are all full, they feel warm. Resi is happy.

She watches Josef and Maria sitting together with the other children at a big table. They seem to have a good time. There is no problem because the children know each other from the road. She looks around, all look so dressed to the nines, although the clothes are partly ripped and the shoes are worn down and have holey soles. They all tried to look good and adequately. In this very moment Resi decides to launch an initiative helping those people sitting at her table today. It is nice to see them happy on Christmas Eve, but what comes then? She would find shelter and work for all of them. There would certainly be enough people in the village who would help her. This is Resi's New Year's resolution. What a pity Doris and Gerda can not see this now, they had to leave to join their respective families.

Both women left big bags for Josef and Maria. They should get them later when going to bed.

They certainly would have agreed with Resi, she would tell them tomorrow.

She is interrupted by a young woman standing in front of her with a stack of plates in her arms and giving her a questioning look. "Oh sorry, I was moony, what did you say?" – "I wanted to know where the kitchen is, I want to clear the table", the young woman asks again.

"Just follow me", Resi tells her, going ahead with two empty dishes. Everybody helps clearing. Dishes are put in the dishwasher, coffee and hot chocolate is made; cups, milk, sugar and bowls with cookies are brought to the dining room. Mineral water and sweets are prepared for the children. Resi decides to start with the gift giving to occupy the children.

She goes in the living room, opens the big double wing door and rings the little bell. First the children do not notice, till one of the boys shouts: "Look, plenty of gifts under the Christmas tree. How beautiful it is!" This is the "go", they all rush to the tree, stop right before it and stare at the huge pile of beautifully wrapped gifts, each by one with a name tag, due to Alois' information. The children turn around, look at their parents, then at Resi and Richard, until Richard says: "Go ahead, get the gifts, but not too wild!"

The parents are standing in the double wing door and watch the children. There is an incredible glance in the children's eyes. The first child arrives with his parcel. "This is for you Mummy." The 10 year-old girl shoves it in her face. "This is not possible, please put it back", the woman says. "But here is your name on it", the little girl pouts. The woman takes the parcel, turns and looks at Resi. "Well, there is something for everyone, even for the adults", Resi answers.

Some of the women cry. They did not expect to see their children so joyous and happy. There are also gifts for Josef and Maria, they are completely stoked. Josef comes to Resi and Richard, hugs both and stammers with tears in his eyes: "Aunt Resi, uncle Richard, I want to thank you for what you did for us. No matter what happens, we will never forget you. Look how Maria radiates. She never really celebrated Christmas in her life. God bless you always", he brings his acceptance speech precociously to an end and turns to his sister.

Resi has to brace herself. She was astonished of what the eight year-old child said. What a great child he was. In this very moment she knows she is doing the right thing. So does Richard, he cannot resist any more and resolves to make those children happy.

Resi takes the small bell and rings it resolutely. "So I think it's now up to the adults to unpack their gifts", she says loud enough to be heard from everywhere. It is the same spectacle as before with the children – glance and tears in the eyes, they cannot believe their fortune.

They all sing a Christmas song to thank Resi and Richard, then they thank them individually. Everybody is happy this evening.

"Here still is one parcel under the tree with Resi's name on it", one of the children shouts. Richard smiles: "So let's see what the Christ Child brought to Resi." It is a new angel for the tree top. Resi is delighted that Richard thought of it. „Maria, do you want to put the angel on the top of the tree? It will just be perfect", she asks the little girl. Richard picks her up. She has some difficulties but then manages to place the angel. All clap their hands. The angel is so beautiful, a worthy replacement for the broken one. Richard is such a darling!

The evening comes to its end. One by one the guests bid farewell and go to sleep in a bed or on one of the prepared couches. It is something very special for these people to sleep washed in a clean bed in a warm room, it did not happen very often.

When Resi puts Josef and Maria to bed, the children discover the big bags. Although they almost fall asleep, they unpack them and realize that this year the Christmas Child meant it ever so well. Resi covers the children. She wants to read a story to them but they are already sleeping. She caresses their heads and goes back to Richard.

They both are too agitated to sleep and decide to go for a walk. They put their thick fur coats on and leave the castle. The inner court is particularly beautiful this night, the moonlight bathes everything in a magic glance. It is ever so peaceful.

"Resi, I thought it over. You are right, we will accommodate the children. I will do everything I can to make them happy. We will be good surrogate parents." Resi takes him in her arms without saying a word. It is the most beautiful present she could get from him for Christmas. Even the angel on the top of the tree is pale in comparison.

They stop at the archway and look to the sky full of blinking stars, they never saw such a starry sky before. Then they cannot believe their eyes. A white mist appears in the sky out of which appears an angel in a white garment and golden hair. The angel smiles at them and disappears as quickly as it had come.

A shooting star seems to fall down on the earth. In this very moment Resi and Richard know that everything will turn out right. They got a message from heaven. None of them talk about the angel not knowing whether the other also saw it. Both believe that their fantasy played a trick on them. Did it? They speak a prayer together and go back in the house.

The next morning everybody gets up very early. The women help Resi in the kitchen to clear up from last evening and prepare breakfast together. They are in a good mood, but feel a drop of bitterness as they will soon have to leave.

It has been snowing for hours, more and more snow is piling up. Richard takes Resi outside the door. "Look at this, we cannot send anyone away now. We would not even get down the mountain. What are we going to do?" Richard worries. „We keep them all here. Somehow we will manage it", Resi answers.

They go back inside to inform everyone. "You can't leave, we did not have so much snow for years. We have to control if we have enough to eat for all of us, otherwise we will have to make things up as we go. Tomorrow we will see. Do you agree?" Richard asks all the attendees.

The young woman named Jasmin who cleared the table the evening before gets up.

„Resi, Richard, we are overwhelmed by such a grace of charity, we cannot thank you enough. But we don't want to overstay your welcome." The others agree, nodding their heads. Resi gets up, her strong voice shows that she does not admit any protest, and sets them straights. "You will all stay here. It's Christmas, it is chilly cold outside and we are snowed in. Nobody has the idea of hitting the road. We will make nametags to better learn each other's names, treat each other as friends and spend the nicest holidays of our life together. I propose the women check how far we get with the eatables. The men might play with the children and if it stops snowing they could go for a snowball fight in the court. By no means you will go back to the street with the children. Did you get me?", Resi asks everybody around.

They all agree and again Jasmin rises to speak. "Fine then, if we don't put you out, we'll stay. But only if we can help cleaning and preparing the meal. And you will also let us clean the floors and toilet. Did you get me Resi?" Jasmin smiles. „That's okay, I even would appreciate it. We will surely spend a wonderful day together", Resi rejoices.

Maria wears her new dress again, Resi arranges her blond hair to a ponytail.

The glance of her big blue eyes makes Resi happy and she asks her whether she already tried all the clothes and if they fit. "Yes, everything fits, also the ones out of the big bag. And Josef also tried his' and all fits well", she answers. – "Good. But put on trousers and boots before you go outside", Resi reminds her. "I will", she shouts before joining the other children.

Josef sits in front of the Christmas tree and looks very sad, his brown eyes tear up. Resi takes him in her arms without a word and caresses his head. Some time later Josef calms down. "It's all right again", he says. Resi caresses his chubby cheeks. „You know Josef, sometimes you have to cry, and then you feel better. Don't be ashamed!" Josef nods, takes the handkerchief she gives him and joins Maria.

Resi is thoughtful, it gets more to him than to Maria, at least for the moment. She will have to keep an eye on him. But no time to sing the blues, she has to go on.

While the women clear the tables and make the beds, Resi gives a phone call to Alois from her office. "Merry Christmas, Alois! – "Same to you Resi, tell me how things pan out!" – "Very good, it was wonderful and we have to keep them all here because of the weather." – "That's what we thought. We are also blocked down here.

Peter is on gritting service, he is unable to cope the piles of snow. The meteorological service says we have not had so much for fifteen years", Alois informs her. "We also heard about it. Richard got a call a while ago. The castle will remain closed tomorrow because of the weather. If it does not change our guests will stay one more day", Resi answers. "We would appreciate your help, I'm afraid we don't have enough to eat and we also need mineral water.

I will call Anton right away to make him prepare something, buns and bread would be great. Could you ask Peter if he takes the things up with the plough?" Resi begs him. "And we need sleeping berths. They cannot sleep outside with this weather, we all know what happened. They want to protect their children and freeze to death. We cannot let it happen once more."

"You are right. I try to manage it till tomorrow. I'm going to stir the whole village into action, count on me. We initially wanted to go to see you but there is no chance, forget about it. We will meet when it is trafficable again. Say hello to everybody from my part and have a nice day." Before the connection is interrupted Resi still hears him shouting: "Gerda, we've got something to do!"

Resi phones to all the drivers who were to bring the guest down to the village today, and tells them that they would be called again when it's time. Then she calls Alois. "Merry Christmas, Alois", she says to her old friend. "Are you snowed in?", he asks immediately. „That's why I'm calling, Anton, we need your help". – „They all stay with you", he asks. That is it, and we don't have enough to eat. Could you go to your shop and prepare something? Alois will tell Peter to bring it to us.

"Sure, tell me what you need"; Alois agrees. "I need cheese, cold cuts, butter, potatoes, some meat and vegetables, and if possible some drinks. Alois will provide bread and cake." Resi hopes not to forget anything. „And some fruit Anton, this will be perfect".

Anton and Gerda are already packing. Peter should come half an hour later. Gerda puts bread, buns and cake in a box, Alois adds coffee, chocolate powder and ten liters of milk. They already called some people of the village for help. Everybody agrees to give all what is not really needed and it shows to be a big lot. All donations are brought to Alois where Peter fetches the boxes. Alois is satisfied, everybody in the village took part.

It was a real good community when someone needed help. He would not want to live anywhere else. He decides to go up together with Peter in order to check everything.

In the castle they hear the plough arriving. The men go to help carrying the boxes. Alois takes a bag Gerda gave him and joins Resi who is again pottering around in the kitchen. She welcomes him: "Hello Alois, nice to see you. Where is Gerda?" – „On the phone with the mayor and the homeless hostel in Füssen in order to find shelter. She maybe will come this evening. Peter cleared and sanded the road when coming up, and will do it again when going down. The way should be more or less trafficable again" he informs. " How reassuring. Something could happen and then you can't get away, that's no good feeling", Rosi answers. "It's fantastic Gerda took over the shelter question. Nobody could do it but her." Resi is confident.

After a cup of coffee Peter an Alois go back to the village. It stopped snowing and the men could go outside with the children for a snowball fight. One hour later they come back exhausted and chilled to the bone.

After the meal the children go for a siesta. The men visit the castle and the women prepare everything to make cookies with the children later on.

Then they sit down in the living room, have tea and cookies and talk. Resi wants to hear every single story. She writes everything down without even knowing why.

She creates a kind of file card of every family writing every person's age, sex, professional education and the reason why they became homeless. Furthermore hobbies and skills of the adults – some can knit, crochet, sew, wallpaper. Resi writes everything down. She wouldn't have thought that almost all of them got in trouble because of unemployment. In January she would check if she could find some jobs for them.

In the afternoon they make cookies in the kitchen, the children have a lot of fun. The men are sitting in the living room and Richard comes to know something about his guests.

Josef and Maria seem to feel good. They are joyful. Just sometimes when they feel unobserved, the little faces turn sad and the eyes tear up. Resi knows they would miss their parents sadly for a long time. Their parents certainly loved the children very much. Alois told Resi that the parents froze to death when they tried to protect the children from the cold with their bodies. How cruel fate can be.

The children survived the night but lost the parents, that was awful. Resi decides that something as horrible should never happen again.

The dinner is being made in the kitchen, the new eatables are prepared or stored away. The children play together in the living room. The men set the table. Finally everybody is busy when the doorbell rings.

Richard opens and sees Alois, Gerda and the mayor. "How nice visitors, come in", he says to the newcomers. Resi comes out of the kitchen to find out who has the heart to come up so late. She is not surprised to see Alois and Gerda what does the mayor come for? She invites all to take a hot spiced wine in the kitchen. Alois and Gerda prefer to take a coffee and look after the children. The mayor wants to talk in confidence with Resi and Richard.

They go to the office where they can talk in private. Resi has a strange feeling. She wonders if he wants to take Josef and Maria to the orphanage. "Over my dead body", she thinks. But it won't go so far, will it? Resi is nervous, she trembles, starts having a lump in her throat. Richard notices his wife's anxiety and puts his arm around her. "Don't bother Resi, everything will turn out right", he appeases her.

The mayor says: "Resi, first of all I am here because of the children. Your husband came to see me yesterday and asked me to start as soon as possible proceedings concerning the children. This morning I also got a call from Richard for the adoption. And here I am now with good news: as from now you are Josef's and Maria's foster parents. Further good news: I pleaded for the adoption. All the people I had to call for this agreed. I first had some scrupulosity to bother the judge on Christmas day, but that just softened his disposition. It will take a while as we still have to check whether there are any blood relatives, but this removes the last obstacle.

Resi starts crying. She thanks the mayor and flings her arms around Richard's neck. "That's where you went yesterday. Thank you Richard, it means so much to me. I thought you only wanted to fetch Franz." She runs in the living room, gets Maria, spins her around. Then it's Josef's turn. Both are completely dumbfounded. „What's the matter aunt Resi", Josef asks.

„Come here everybody, I've got something to tell you", she shouts. As soon as everybody is around, she spreads the news. Maria comes back to her. She takes her on her arms again. "Aunt Resi, isn't it good news?" she enquires. „Yes it is, it is fantastic", Resi answers.

"But why are you crying?" – „Because I am so happy. This is your home now. If you want you may stay forever with us", Resi explains. „Is it true, we may really stay?" Josef asks once again. "Yes, that's what I'm saying all the time", she shouts out. A real exaltation brakes out. Josef runs to Richard, Maria kisses Resi again and again.

They understood so late because Resi spoke so quickly and her voice cracked while she announced the good news.

Everybody congratulates, thank the mayor and is happy for them. As soon as they all calm down, Alois rises to speak. "Listen everybody, the mayor still has something to say." It takes a moment to get completely silent.

"Dear attendees", he formally starts. "I don't know if it's because of Christmas, or of the sentimental people living here. I got phone calls all morning long and suspect Gerda to have incited it. Whoever it was, he thought I did not deserve a Christmas day. More and more people asked me to do something against homelessness in our village.

It seems the matter cannot wait till after Christmas. They pushed me to take care immediately. I finally did, otherwise I would not have had a minute of rest till New Year.

Well, I found a house belonging to the town which we can make available, but only from December 27th on. Till then all the nice people who called me will give shelter. I now would like to return to my family who came from Switzerland to see me. I will wait for you in the village hall on 27th at half past ten to discuss further measures. As I heard everybody will stay in the castle till tomorrow. The families offering shelter will contact you during the day. You will manage all the rest. And by the way: Resi, Gerda, you will both guarantee for the house. Start thinking it over", the mayor concludes his speech. He leaves wishing a nice holiday to everybody.

The atmosphere this evening is more than words can say. The dinner is delayed accordingly. It is past nine when the children finally all are in bed. Alois and Gerda stay for dinner, everyone thanks effusively, and they also leave. Resi takes Josef and Maria to their temporary room. "I promise when they will all be gone, you will get a real nice room of your own", she apologizes.

"Don't bother aunt Resi. We know that the others need your help. We are not alone in the world at least", Josef appeases her.

Maria puts her little arms around Resi and whispers in her ear: "I love you".

Resi is so touched, these children are really incredible. She kisses them good night. "I also do love you, sleep well", she adds and leaves the room. Richard wants to read a story to them this evening. So she has time to digest all what just happened. She puts her coat on and goes in the inner court. The sky is clear and glancing. Resi stands and looks at it while tears run over her face. She thanks God for being so lucky in her age to have two charming children with her.

When she is fine again she joins the others.

They make plans for the house and plans who is taking over the different tasks. This evening Richard and Resi go happily to bed and wake up rested and refreshed the next morning.

Resi is attracted in the kitchen by the smell of coffee. She does not believe her eyes – breakfast is ready, table set and the children are washed and dressed, even Josef and Maria. Outside it is snowing a little and there is fire in the chimney. "What a beautiful morning", Resi says to herself while she serves herself a cup of coffee.

They spend a relaxed morning and have lunch together. The drivers arrive little by little to take the guests from Castle Neuschwanstein to the village. The farewell is some melancholy.

Jasmin takes Resi in her arm: "Do you know how happy you made us all? Richard and you deserve to be happy. We thank you so much. God bless you", she says and everybody agrees.

They all promise to meet in the village hall the next day. Then the four are alone again.

Resi thinks all have been so satisfied and hard working this year. The beds are cleaned up, the kitchen is nice and tidy, they even dusted and hovered. She only had to store away the covers and wash the bed sheet, then everything would be like it was before. Now it is time to care about Josef and Maria.

They dress nice warm and go for a walk to the bridge "Marienbrücke". "Do you like being here?" Resi begins the conversation. "Very much indeed, although we do miss Mummy and Daddy a lot. But it is better to be here than in an orphanage", Josef answers precociously. "You don't mind us being your foster parents, do you?" Richard asks. "That's great. Will we stay in the castle?" Maria enquires.

„Yes, forever with us in the castle. Well, maybe not forever. The day I will not work here any more, we will move down to the village. But till then we all stay here. However, you will have to follow some rules.

It is not our own Castle, we are only taking care of it.

Therefore, you will never play in the castle. I will show you everything around. You might look at everything when I am with you, but do not go there alone. One more thing: Every day a lot of strangers come here. You will never go with anyone of them, is that clear?" Richard enjoins them.

Both children nod their heads and promise to stick to it. "We promise not to trouble you", Josef says and Maria nods, putting her little hand on her chest.

They have fun in the yard with the children, let them make snow angels and a snowman.

"Now let's go inside, we have to prepare your rooms." The evening is very harmonious. Maria is just sad one moment, but her brother immediately takes her in his arms to comfort her. Resi brings both to bed and tells them a story of Moppel, the dwarf rabbit. The children fall asleep.

The next morning after breakfast Resi and the children go to the village. Richard has to stay in the castle which is open again for visitors.

They go to have a hot chocolate at Alois', from where they want to push on to the mayor.

Gerda has something to tell, having organized a lot for the new house and also talked to the mayor the day before. "So there is an abandoned house in the suburb which belongs to the community. They put it to our disposal if we refurbish it by ourselves and keep it in good nick. In return we don't have to pay any rent for one year. Later on we will have to negotiate. He could not tell me how much it would be, we'll see when the time comes. The refurbishing material will be donated partly by the community and the craftsmen of the village, and also the tools as long as we don't find any in the neighbourhood. Our friends who are willing to help will of course use their own tools", Gerda explains.

Resi cannot believe it. "How could you organize all this in such a short time?" Alois takes over: „Well, you know Gerda. She does not take *I'm not available on Christmas* for an answer."

"Gerda, you are a genius. Go ahead", Resi compliments her friend who answers: "You know Resi, after having spent one evening with the children and their parents I realized how lucky we are. I saw how they enjoyed being with you and what great people they are.

I just knew I had to help. Nobody deserved what happened on Christmas Eve. And it was time to awake our village. Now the solidarity shows and we can look ahead."

The village Hohenschwangau had always had its own philosophy. You had to help the one who needs it. During the last year it had fallen behind, nobody knows why. Maybe because of all those tourists invading the village daily. Everyone was concerned with his own affairs. This would change now. „It seems they get back to altruism", Resi says to herself.

It is time to go to the community hall. Alois keeps the children with him whereas Gerda and Resi set forth. A huge crowd is waiting in front of the hall. Everybody is there, even neighbours want to help.

"It got around quickly"; Resi says to Gerda. "Let's go". The two women go ahead, followed by the crowd. The mayor looks astonished and takes a deep breath, he did not expect so many people. Then he clears his throat. At this sign, everybody keeps quiet.

"I want to welcome you all and am happy so many people are here", he begins his speech. "Before we start I want to call Resi Brunner, there is something she has to do first".

He gives her the printed form confirming that they are Josef's and Maria's foster parents.

She signs right away, Richard will do so later. Everyone claps, it is official from now on. Resi is at all smiles.

"Let's get to the other point, the building in the suburb." He announces once again the conditions Gerda already mentioned". I issued a list with the material the community is donating. You have to take care of the rest. Once a month someone of the administration will take a look at the building's state. Gerda and Resi, would you please sign here. You guarantee for the house as I already mentioned." His speech was clear for everyone. Should something go wrong with the house, they would be hold liable for. But the women trust the people who would move in.

Jasmin pipes up, she seems to have taken over the leadership. "Gerda, Resi, mayor and also all attendees, we would like to thank you for trusting us and for the helping hands. We won't disappoint you. Should ever one of you need help, count on us. God bless you all." The others nod in agreement.

The mayor ceremonially hands over the keys for the house to Resi, then they bid farewell and leave.

Everybody celebrates and hugs Resi and Gerda.

Once all together visited the house, Jasmin and Resi distribute the tasks to the different persons. The men take their cars to get the material and tools. The others start decluttering.

Back in the bakery, Gerda picks up some cleaning agent and Resi looks after the children and calls Richard on the phone. He should return later on to sign the papers and they could then all celebrate the happening together.

Resi and the children go to buy even more cloths. Josef is to go to school from January on and Maria to the kidsgarden. They would need more warm cloths to play outside. Then they go to a toyshop, as they need games for the evenings, painting books and colouring pencils. Resi would care for the school supplies after New Year; she is busy with other things now.

Richard gets all excited when hearing about the signature story and promises to join her as soon as possible.

There is a hustle and bustle in the village. People walk around with paint buckets, wallpaper rolls, fabric and many more. Somebody enters the bakery. They had issued a list with furniture someone has in the basement: beds, sofas, armchairs, tables, chairs and wardrobes.

The list also contains bed sheet, curtains, tableware and cutlery. The owner of the household supply store comes and offers to give cooking pots and frying pans for every family. The children are done looking through and packing together their clothes and games. Alois stores the boxes. Anton from the supermarket wants to do the basic catering. First telephone calls come from the town of Füssen. A big fund-raiser had been started which brought woollen blankets, covers, pillows and kitchen equipment. Shopping vouchers would help the families to get over the first two weeks. Resi and Gerda had never expected such an immense feedback. It seems that the action was announced by radio, more and more calls and donations arrive. Alois has to manage all, no doubt he would, even for transport and interim storage facilities. Resi wants to tell the good news to the others.

In the afternoon Alois and Richard go to the house to see how works are going on and are astonished. It already is decluttered, the first rooms are painted, a woman is sewing curtains with a sewing machine. The toilets are removed and being replaced by new ones. "It's running like clockwork", Alois shouts to the men working who acclaim the newcomers. Richard adds with his strong voice: "I just met the mayor. The papers are signed.

Josef, Maria, Resi and me are a real family now. We want to celebrate it. Alois and me brought buns, cake and Bavarian meat loaf, we also have coffee and mineral water for everybody."

Josef and Maria look at each other, what did he say? They are a real family? In the very moment they get the meaning they run to jump on them. Maria is screaming so much that her little voice almost cracks. Everybody rejoices and grant with pleasure the luck to the children.

Thanks to all the helpers from the village most of the work is done in the evening. The next day they would have to acquire the rest of the furniture and achieve the chicken-feed. It has been an eventful day. Everybody is tired and exhausted. As they want to go home six more unexpected visitors arrive, all businessmen from the village and the town of Füssen. They offer six jobs, from January on five men and one woman would be employed. The day couldn't have ended better.

Jasmin chimes in and thanks in the name of all for so much charity. "You did everything possible to get us on the right way. From now on we will manage it ourselves. We have become a strong community during the last days and this will remain. We even don't want to imagine what would have happened if we had not got so much help.

You all arranged a Christmas Miracle we will never forget." Jasmin bows to the benefactors. Then she joins Resi, takes her in her arms and says: "Should you ever need help, let me know." – "This is not our merit and it is no miracle. Just coincidences happening at the same time", Resi answers. "Coincidences – giving shelter on Christmas Eve to two children named Josef and Maria, you call this coincidence? No my dear, it is a real Christmas Miracle", Jasmin insists. All attendees are giving thunderous applause.

From that day on this story has been told on Christmas Eve in every living room, and till today it is considered as

"The Christmas Miracle of Castle Neuschwanstein".

Just one more thing:

For quite some time I have been trying to help persons who got in trouble. Unfortunately there are sometimes people who take advantage of it. However my device is: Those who really need help should not suffer from it. I admit defeat when it occurs and continue nevertheless.

This made me write this book

"The Christmas Miracle of Castle Neuschwanstein".

In spite of the price increase due to the Euro most of us are able to master their lives. Unfortunately there are quite some fellow men who are not. It is even worse when children are involved.

I am sure we can help those children if everyone of us shows just a little compassion and sympathy. The glance in children's eyes or the sound of children's laugh make us happy. The feeling when you have a little baby in your arms is indescribably. You can see the future and the past in this tiny being.

This warm feeling of luck just flows through your body. We all want every child in this world to have the same chance. Don't we wish that every child grows happily in a family? Why do so many people sit at their hands when the children in our neighbourhood are badly off? I don't ask you to give them any money, just a little compassion: a sandwich, something to drink, some fruit or cookies could work wonders.

It is not about the eatables but about the thoughtfulness you give to the child.

The small gesture shows to someone that he's not alone, he is loved by somebody. Do not stumble through live with your eyes shot, make a child happy.

Let the miracle happen, God and the child will thank you.

I decided to donate a part of the revenues of this book to the children in our town. What do you plan to do?

I wish you a lucky life.

Marion Wittrowski

The Author

Marion Wittrowski, born in 1958, wrote this book to show how wonderful helping other people can be. She appeals to all people to look around. It is not always important to give money. Offer some help from time to time to an old lady in your neighbourship, smile at the people on the road or in the bus. It is so easy to give just a little. Even your day would change if someone smiled at you in the morning.

This book was written to get attentive.

Be attentive.

Bavarian
Castle Neuschwanstein

King Ludwig II of Bavaria

Biography

Born on 25th August 1845 in Castle Nymphenburg

King of Bavaria 1864 – 1886

Died on 13th June 1886

Even before he died, the king had already become something of a legend.

"I want to remain an eternal mystery of myself and others", Ludwig once told his governess, and it is this mysterious element that still fascinates people today.

Neuschwanstein Castle is a 19th-century Gothic Revival palace on a rugged hill above the village of Hohenschwangau near Füssen in southwest Bavaria, Germany. The palace was commissioned by Ludwig II of Bavaria as a retreat and as a homage to Richard Wagner. The palace was intended as a personal refuge for the reclusive king, but it was opened to the paying public immediately after his death in 1886.[1] Since then over 60 million people have visited Neuschwanstein Castle.[2] More than 1.3 million people visit annually, with up to 6,000 per day in the summer.[3]

The palace has appeared prominently in several movies and was the inspiration for Disneyland's Sleeping Beauty Castle[4] and later, similar structures.

The municipality of <u>Schwangau</u> lies at an elevation of 800 m (2,620 ft) at the south west border of the German state of Bavaria. Its surroundings are characterized by the transition between the Alpine foothills in the south (towards the nearby Austrian border) and a hilly landscape in the north that appears flat by comparison. In the Middle Ages, three castles overlooked the village.

One was called Schwanstein Castle.[nb 1] In 1832, Ludwig's father King Maximilian II of Bavaria bought its ruins to replace them by the comfortable neo-Gothic palace known as Hohenschwangau Castle.

Finished in 1837, the palace became his family's summer residence, and his elder son Ludwig (born 1845) spent a large part of his childhood here.

In the 19th century only ruins remained of the medieval twin castles, but those of Hinterhohenschwangau served as a lookout place known as Sylphenturm.[5]

The ruins above the family palace were known to the crown prince from his excursions. He first sketched one of them in his diary in 1859.[6] When the young king came to power in 1864, the construction of a new palace in place of the two ruined castles became the first in his series of palace building projects.[7] Ludwig himself called the new palace New Hohenschwangau Castle – only after his death was it renamed *Neuschwanstein*.[8]

The confusing result is that Hohenschwangau and Schwanstein have effectively swapped names: Hohenschwangau Castle replaced the ruins of Schwanstein Castle, and Neuschwanstein Castle replaced the ruins of the two Hohenschwangau Castles.

At the time of Ludwig's death the palace was far from complete. The external structures of the Gatehouse and the Palace were mostly finished, but the Rectangular Tower was still scaffolded. Work on the Bower had not started, but was completed in simplified form by 1892, without the planned female saints figures. The Knights' House was also simplified. In Ludwig's plans the columns in the Knights' House gallery were held as tree trunks and the capitals as the corresponding crowns. Only the foundations existed for the core piece of the palace complex: a keep of 90 metres height planned in the upper courtyard, resting on a three-nave chapel. This was not realized,[9] and a connection wing between the Gatehouse and the Bower saw the same fate.[15] Plans for a castle garden with terraces and a fountain west of the Palace were also abandoned after the king's death.

The interior of the royal living space in the palace was mostly completed in 1886; the lobbies and corridors were painted in a simpler style by 1888.[14] The *Moorish Hall* desired by the king (and planned below the Throne Hall) was not realized any more than the so-called *Knights' Bath*, which, modelled after the Knights' Bath in the Wartburg, was intended to render homage to the knights' cult as a medieval baptism bath.

A *Bride Chamber* in the Bower (after a location in *Lohengrin*),[10] guest rooms in the first and second floor of the Palace and a great banquet hall were further abandoned projects.[13] In fact, a complete development of Neuschwanstein had never even been planned, and at the time of the king's death there was not a utilization concept for numerous rooms.[11]

When Ludwig II died in 1886, Neuschwanstein was still incomplete. The king never intended to make the palace accessible to the public.[12] But no more than six weeks after the king's death the regent Luitpold ordered the palace opened to paying visitors. The administrators of Ludwig's estate managed to balance the construction debts by 1899.[16] From then until World War I, Neuschwanstein was a stable and lucrative source of revenue for the House of Wittelsbach, indeed Ludwig's castles were probably the single largest income source earned by the Bavarian royal family in the last years prior to 1914. To guarantee a smooth course of visits, some rooms and the court buildings were finished first. Initially the visitors were allowed to move freely in the palace, causing the furniture to wear quickly.

References:

nb1. ^ <u>*a*</u> <u>*b*</u> Bayerisches Staatsministerium der Finanzen 2005

2. ^ <u>*a*</u> <u>*b*</u> Bayerisches Staatsministerium der Finanzen 2009

3. ^ <u>*a*</u> <u>*b*</u> Bayerisches Staatsministerium der Finanzen 2008

4. ^ Smith & 2008 pp. 79,83

5. ^ Petzet & Hojer 1991, p. 4

6. ^ Rauch 1991, p. 8

7. ^ <u>*a*</u> <u>*b*</u> <u>*c*</u> Blunt 1970, p. 110

8. ^ <u>*a*</u> <u>*b*</u> Petzet & Hojer 1991, p. 46

9. ^ <u>*a*</u> <u>*b*</u> Petzet & Hojer 1991, p. 12
10. ^ <u>*a*</u> <u>*b*</u> Petzet & Hojer 1991, p. 9
11. ^ <u>*a*</u> <u>*b*</u> Rauch 1991, p. 14
12. ^ <u>*a*</u> <u>*b*</u> <u>*c*</u> <u>*d*</u> <u>*e*</u> Petzet & Hojer 1991, p. 19

13. ^ <u>*a*</u> <u>*b*</u> <u>*c*</u> <u>*d*</u> Rauch 1991, p. 13
14. ^ <u>*a*</u> <u>*b*</u> Petzet & Hojer 1991, p. 26
15. ^ Petzet & Hojer 1991, p. 22
16. ^ Rauch 1991, p. 16